Clifford THE BIG RED DOG®

TEACHER'S PETS

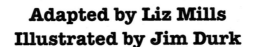
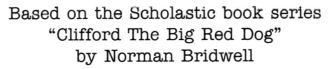

Adapted by Liz Mills
Illustrated by Jim Durk

Based on the Scholastic book series
"Clifford The Big Red Dog"
by Norman Bridwell

From the television script
"Teacher's Pet" by Lois Becker

SCHOLASTIC INC.

New York   Toronto   London   Auckland   Sydney
Mexico City   New Delhi   Hong Kong   Buenos Aires

ISBN 0-439-65039-9

12 11 10 9 8 7 6 5 4 3 2 1   4 5 6 7 8 9/0
Printed in the U.S.A.
First Scholastic printing, April 2004

24

"Welcome to doggy school, everyone," said Brittany Spaniel. "We're going to have lots of fun together!

"First, I want each of you to roll over.
Cleo, you go first."

Cleo rolled.

And rolled.

And rolled!

"That's enough rolling, Cleo!" said Brittany, laughing. "Well done!"

"Now it's your turn, Clifford."
When Clifford rolled, the ground
shook. Everyone went down with him.

"Wow, Clifford. You make a *big* impression!" said Brittany, standing up.

"Mac, you're next," said Brittany.

But Mac wouldn't budge. No matter what Brittany did, he refused to roll.

"Would you do it for a treat?" she asked.

In one motion, Mac did a roll,
sat up, and gobbled his treat.

Brittany laughed. "That was very
good, Mac.

"Ready, T-Bone?"

At first, T-Bone was too nervous. Then he crouched down,

did one careful roll,

and smiled.

"That was just fine, T-Bone," said
Brittany as she turned to the other dogs.

T-Bone's smile went away.

Just fine? he thought. *But I did a good
roll. Why didn't she like it? Maybe
tomorrow will be better.*

The next day, Brittany taught a new trick. "Now, I want everyone to fetch this ball. Clifford, you go first."

Brittany threw the ball as far as she could.

Clifford ran and ran, over the trees and into the ocean.

When he returned with the ball, Brittany smiled. "That was excellent, Clifford."

"Cleo, you're next," said Brittany.

Cleo brought back the ball.

And then a newspaper.

And then a stick!

"Cleo, you're doing very well!" said
Brittany encouragingly.

"Your turn, Mac."

Once again, Mac didn't move.

"Okay, Mac, how about another treat?"
asked Brittany, smiling.

Away Mac ran, after the ball. He dropped it at Brittany's feet and gobbled up the treat.

When T-Bone's turn came, he
quickly brought the ball back to
Brittany, panting hopefully.

"Thank you, T-Bone. That was just
fine," said Brittany.

Later T-Bone said, "Clifford, I'm trying my hardest, but she only says I'm doing just fine."

"Believe in yourself, T-Bone," said Clifford. "We all think you're doing great!"

The other dogs barked in agreement.

At the end of the week, Brittany said, "You've all done wonderfully. I'll see you at graduation tomorrow."

T-Bone gulped. *Graduation?*

"I want the biggest trophy ever!" said Cleo.

"I want Emily Elizabeth to come see me,"
said Clifford.

"I want lots and lots of treats!" said Mac.

"I just want to graduate," said T-Bone quietly.

"All my dogs did very well this week," said Brittany.

"The award for the most enthusiastic student goes to Cleo!

"The award for making the biggest impression goes to Clifford!

"The award for the best tricks for treats goes to Mac!"

"And the award for the hardest-working student who always tried his best goes to… T-Bone!"

And that made T-Bone feel just fine!